Dear Parents and Educators,

Welcome to Penguin Young Readers! As parents and educators, you know that each child develops at his or her own pace—in terms of speech, critical thinking, and, of course, reading. Penguin Young Readers recognizes this fact. As a result, each Penguin Young Readers book is assigned a traditional easy-to-read level (1–4) as well as a Guided Reading Level (A–P). Both of these systems will help you choose the right book for your child. Please refer to the back of each book for specific leveling information. Penguin Young Readers features esteemed authors and illustrators, stories about favorite characters, fascinating nonfiction, and more!

Nina, Nina and the Copycat Ballerina	LEVEL **2** GUIDED READING LEVEL **G**

This book is perfect for a **Progressing Reader** who:
- can figure out unknown words by using picture and context clues;
- can recognize beginning, middle, and ending sounds;
- can make and confirm predictions about what will happen in the text; and
- can distinguish between fiction and nonfiction.

Here are some **activities** you can do during and after reading this book:
- Read the Pictures: Use the pictures to tell the story. Have the child go through the book, retelling the story just by looking at the pictures.
- Make Connections: In this story, Nina does not like it when the new Nina copies her. Discuss a time when a friend did something you did not like. How did you feel and why? What did you say to your friend?

Remember, sharing the love of reading with a child is the best gift you can give!

—Bonnie Bader, EdM
    Penguin Young Readers program

*Penguin Young Readers are leveled by independent reviewers applying the standards developed by Irene Fountas and Gay Su Pinnell in *Matching Books to Readers: Using Leveled Books in Guided Reading*, Heinemann, 1999.

For Natalie and Caitlin—JOC

To the biggest copycat I know—
my sister Vicki—DD

Penguin Young Readers
Published by the Penguin Group
Penguin Group (USA) Inc., 375 Hudson Street, New York, New York 10014, USA
Penguin Group (Canada), 90 Eglinton Avenue East, Suite 700, Toronto, Ontario M4P 2Y3, Canada
(a division of Pearson Penguin Canada Inc.)
Penguin Books Ltd, 80 Strand, London WC2R 0RL, England
Penguin Ireland, 25 St Stephen's Green, Dublin 2, Ireland (a division of Penguin Books Ltd)
Penguin Group (Australia), 707 Collins Street, Melbourne, Victoria 3008, Australia
(a division of Pearson Australia Group Pty Ltd)
Penguin Books India Pvt Ltd, 11 Community Centre, Panchsheel Park, New Delhi—110 017, India
Penguin Group (NZ), 67 Apollo Drive, Rosedale, Auckland 0632, New Zealand
(a division of Pearson New Zealand Ltd)
Penguin Books (South Africa), Rosebank Office Park,
181 Jan Smuts Avenue, Parktown North 2193, South Africa
Penguin China, B7 Jiaming Center, 27 East Third Ring Road North,
Chaoyang District, Beijing 100020, China

Penguin Books Ltd, Registered Offices: 80 Strand, London WC2R 0RL, England

Text copyright © 2000 by Jane O'Connor. Illustrations copyright © 2000 by DyAnne DiSalvo.
All rights reserved. First published in 2000 by Grosset & Dunlap, an imprint of Penguin Group (USA) Inc.
Published in 2013 by Penguin Young Readers, an imprint of Penguin Group (USA) Inc.,
345 Hudson Street, New York, New York 10014. Manufactured in China.

Library of Congress Control Number: 99048179

ISBN 978-0-448-42151-3

10 9 8 7 6 5 4 3 2 1

ALWAYS LEARNING

PEARSON

Nina, Nina and the Copycat Ballerina

WITHDRAWN

by Jane O'Connor
illustrated by DyAnne DiSalvo

Penguin Young Readers
An Imprint of Penguin Group (USA) Inc.

This is Nina.

And this is Nina, too.

She is new at dance class.

Miss Dawn says, "I will call you

Nina One and Nina Two."

Nina Two is a good dancer.

And she is nice.

She helps Nina One with her splits.

After class,

she always shares

her candy bar.

But there is

one bad thing

about Nina Two.

She is a copycat.

She gets the same

leotard as Nina One,

the same

leg warmers,

and the same

dance bag

with a key chain.

7

"Look!" Nina Two says one day.

She takes off her hat.

"My hair is like yours!"

says Nina Two.

"Now we can be like twins."

Nina One does not say

anything.

She does not want

to be like twins.

She wants to be just herself—

Nina.

That day Miss Dawn

tells the class about

the next dance show.

"Each of you will make up

your very own dance."

Nina is excited.

In the car she tells her mom,

"We have to think up

all the steps.

The dance can be a solo.

That means you do it

by yourself.

Or it can be a duet—

that means you do it

with another kid."

At home Nina thinks

about her dance.

Yes! She has a cool idea.

She finds an old wand.

She tapes on ribbons.

She will do a solo.

She will be a rainbow!

At the next class,

Jody and Ann work on a duet.

They are puppets on strings.

Eric is doing a solo.

He is a karate guy.

He does kicks and twirls

and a backflip!

Nina works on her dance.

She runs and leaps.

Then she runs and leaps

some more.

"Very nice," says Miss Dawn.

"But try to put more steps

in your dance."

In the dressing room,

Nina Two comes up to her.

"I'm not sure

what my dance will be.

Maybe I will be a rainbow, too."

All of a sudden Nina gets mad.

Very mad.

"No!" she says.

"That's *my* idea.

And you can't copy it."

Nina Two's face gets all red.

Nina One gets her dance bag

and walks away.

All week Nina tries to make

her dance better.

She does not think

about the other Nina.

She sees herself

in the mirror.

She tries twirls.

No good.

She tries splits.

No good.

She ends up poking herself

in the tummy.

It does not hurt that much.

But Nina starts to cry.

"My dance is dumb,"

she says to her mom.

Then she cries harder.

She tells Mom about Nina Two.

"I feel bad.

I was mean.

But she is such a copycat."

Mom understands.

"Tell her that you're sorry.

But also tell her how you feel."

Nina wants to.

But that is hard . . . even harder

than doing a good split.

She waits for Nina Two

at dance class.

"I am sorry I yelled," she says.

"I *like* you.

It's just—"

Nina Two stops her.

"It's okay.

I am sorry, too.

I will stop being a big copycat."

They both laugh.

Nina Two smiles.

"Too bad I can't do

a dance about a copycat."

Later in class Nina Two

comes up to Nina One.

She has an idea for a dance—

a duet.

Nina One thinks

the idea is great.

It will be cooler than her

dumb rainbow dance.

So they talk to Miss Dawn.

They spend the day together.
Nina One has good ideas
for the costumes.

Nina Two has good ideas
for the dance steps.

They work hard together.

They have fun together, too.

At last it is the day of the show.

Nina One and Nina Two

do their duet.

Nina One is a black cat.

Nina Two is the same black cat

in a mirror.

They pounce.

They prance.

They paw at each other.

At the end

everybody claps and claps.

Sometimes it is fun

to be a copycat!